Scary Fairies

Scary Fairies

Written by
DUGALD STEER
Illustrated by
PATRICIA LUDLOW

THE MILLBROOK PRESS
Brookfield, Connecticut

At the farthest end of the garden path,
At night when the moon is out,
Or just outside of the garden gate,
There's something strange about.

It's there that the Scary Fairies hide.
They don't know how to be good,
And how they laugh such wicked laughs
When children get lost in the wood!

The gooseberry bush by the garden fence
Is a place you should never go,
For down by the roots of the greenest shoots,
The fairy babies grow.

Now fairy babies are rather fierce,
For up your legs they'll climb,
And pull on your hair and your nose and your ears
A hundred or more at a time!

When your puppy or kitten seems terribly strange,
But looks just the same as before—
When nothing you do can help make them tame,
The fairies have changed them for sure.

You'll know when they bite and they bark and they scratch,
When they claw and they hiss and attack,
The fairies have taken the real ones away,
Who knows when you'll get them back.

A fairy ring is a wonderful thing,
Oh, wouldn't a dance be fun?
But that's where toadstool fairies live,
So if I were you, I'd run!

They fiercely guard their woodland homes.
They've got a magic trick
That makes you jump and bounce about
And dance until you're sick!

Honey is sweet, so lovely to eat,
But if you should find a hive,
Don't leave it too late—just make an escape,
If you want to get home by five.

It could be a fairy hive you've found
All full of fairy bees—
A swarm of these beastly beasts will swoop
And sting you as much as they please!

There's a fairy who looks like a twisted oak.
He isn't a nice one at all.
He'll stick out a gnarly, raggedy root,
To trip you up and you'll fall.

Into a thicket of nettles you'll crash,
Or into a bramble patch—
Who knows how you'll ever get out again,
And, oh, how those brambles will scratch!

There's a fairy who'll push you into the mud.
He'll cover your clothes with goo.
You'll never be able to wash it off,
As it sticks like slimy glue.

He'll throw ripe berries and rotten fruit.
He'll pull you along in the grass.
Until your clothes are covered in stains,
He will not let you pass.

A fairy in black with a broom and a cat
May call out your name as you walk,
And kindly ask you the time of the year,
But do not stop to talk.

She'll lock you away in a hideous hole;
She'll hide you away underground;
She'll feed you on maggots
and beetles and worms.
It could be hours before you're found!

Don't look in a pool by the light of moon—
It's truly a terrible sight.
For out of the deep a fairy will creep
To give you a horrible fright.

He'll reach out and grab you; he'll clutch and he'll claw;
He'll gnaw and he'll gnash with his teeth.
He might even call you some really bad names,
As he slides back down underneath.

A crooked old fairy with only three teeth
May invite you home for some stew.
But don't ever go, 'cause you never know...
The stew could turn out to be you!

Just say, "Not today!" and walk right away,
Even though you are hungry and hot.
You're sticky and icky, in need of a bath,
But you don't want it to be in her pot!

With so many terrible fairies around
It might seem unsafe to go out—
But there's one thing that Scary Fairies don't like
And that's if you whistle or shout.
They cannot stand noise, so if you're afraid,
And you think that you're under a charm,
Just yell or sing out at the top of your voice
And then you will come to no harm.

If you ever thought they were scary at all
You will see that it's all just a sham,
As soon as you laugh or don't look afraid
You'll see how those fairies all scram!
For the truth of it is, and it's plain as your face,
More simple than counting to two,
The scariest fairies that ever there were
Are much, much more frightened of you.

A TEMPLAR BOOK

First published in the United States in 1997

by The Millbrook Press, Inc., 2 Old New Milford Road, Brookfield, CT 06804

Devised and produced by The Templar Company plc,

Pippbrook Mill, London Road, Dorking, Surrey, RH4 1JE, Great Britain

Copyright © 1997 by The Templar Company plc

Holograms created and manufactured by Opsec International plc, U.K.

Library of Congress Cataloging-in-Publication Data

Steer, Dug.

Scary fairies/by Dugald Steer: illustrations by Patricia Ludlow.

p.   cm.

Summary: Introduces mischievous fairy babies, tricky toadstool

fairies, nasty fairies who trip people and cover their clothes with

goo, and other unpleasant supernatural creatures.

ISBN 0-7613-0258-1 (lib. bdg.).–– ISBN 0-7613-0298-0 (trade)

[1. Fairies––Fiction. 2. Stories in rhyme.] I. Ludlow,

Patricia, ill. II. Title.

PZ8.2.8135Sg 1997

[E]––dc21   97–12757

                                                           CIP

                                                           AC